D1090365

MINI CLASSICS

THE
STEADFAST
TIN SOLDIER

RETOLD BY STEPHANIE LASLETT
ILLUSTRATED BY HELEN SMITH

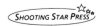

SHOOTING STAR PRESS

TITLES IN SERIES I AND III OF THE MINI CLASSICS INCLUDE:

SERIES I

SERIES III

This edition printed for:
Shooting Star Press, Inc.
230 Fifth Avenue–Suite 1212,
New York, NY 10001

Shooting Star Press books are available at special
discounts for bulk purchases for sales promotions,
premiums, fund-raising, or educational use. Special
editions or book excerpts can also be created to
specification. For details contact: Special Sales
Director, Shooting Star Press, Inc., 230 Fifth Avenue,
Suite 1212, New York, New York 10001.

ISBN 1-56924-238-0

Printed and bound in Great Britain.

There were once upon a time five-and-twenty tin soldiers — all brothers, for they were made out of the same old tin spoon. Dressed in a smart red uniform, each one carried a gun upon his shoulder and looked straight ahead with a brave and steady gaze. They lay side by side in a wooden box and the first words that they heard when the lid was lifted off, were, "Hurray, tin soldiers!"

Looking down upon them was an excited little boy clapping his hands at the sight of his new birthday present. Carefully the boy began to set out the soldiers on the table. Each tin soldier was exactly like the other in every way, except just one. He had been made last of all when the tin ran out and so he had only one leg, but there he stood as firm and steadfast on his one leg as the others did on two.

This is the Tin Soldier
who became famous, as
you will soon see.

As the soldiers stood straight and tall, glad to be freed from their box at last, they could see something else upon the table. Close by was a pretty little castle made of cardboard. It had proper windows so

they could look through
straight into the rooms.
 In front of the castle
was a lake made from a
tiny mirror, surrounded
by green trees. White
wax swans swam on the
still surface of the water,
admiring their reflections.

Now this was all very pretty, but the most beautiful thing of all was a sweet little lady who stood in the open doorway of the castle. She was made of paper, but wore a soft white dress of the finest muslin.

A scarf of narrow blue
ribbon was draped
around her shoulders
and pinned together at
the front of her bodice
with a glittering rose
brooch made of gold
paper. It was almost as
large as her head!

The little lady stood
beautifully tall and
straight and carried her
arms high above her
head, for she was a
Dancer.

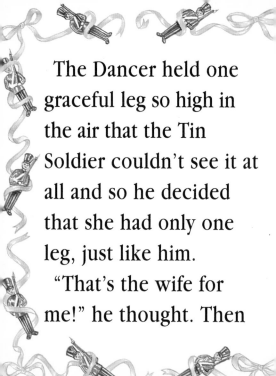

The Dancer held one graceful leg so high in the air that the Tin Soldier couldn't see it at all and so he decided that she had only one leg, just like him.

"That's the wife for me!" he thought. Then

a sad expression crossed his face and he sighed deeply. "But what is the use of trying to win her love. She is so grand and lives in a splendid castle, whilst I have only a box and I have to share that with my twenty four brothers. This is no place for her!" and the poor Tin Soldier sighed again as he gazed at the lovely lady. "But she is so very beautiful! I must at least meet her and say hello." All that day the Soldier

stood tall and straight
behind a snuff box that
lay on the table and
from there he had a
clear view of the dainty
little Dancer, who
continued to stand on
one leg without ever
losing her balance.

When the day was over,
the little boy carefully
packed his Tin Soldiers
away in their box and
didn't notice that one
of them was missing. As
night fell, the dark house
grew still and soon
everyone was fast asleep.

Then it was time for the toys to play! Up they jumped and danced and fought, and merrily laughed and sang.

The Tin Soldiers could hear all the noise and they rattled and jostled against one another for they longed to join in the fun. But no matter how much they shook their box they could not raise the lid and so

had to lie there alone
in the dark, listening to
the other toys having a
wonderful time while
their shadows danced
on the walls.

The nutcrackers played at leap-frog and the slate pencil ran all over the slate! There was such a noise that the canary woke up and began to chatter and sing to them all, and in poetry too!

The only two toys who did not stir from their places were the Tin Soldier and the little Dancer. She remained on tip-toe, with both arms outstretched; he stood steadfastly on his one leg and his eyes never left her face.

Suddenly, in a dark corner of the nursery, the tall grandfather clock struck twelve, and crack! off flew the lid of the snuff box — but there was no snuff inside, only a little

black imp who popped
up just like a jack-in-
the-box.

"Hello, Tin Soldier!"
said the imp. "Why are
you looking at the little
Dancer? Don't you
know that it's rather
rude to stare?"

33

But the Tin Soldier took no notice. He acted as if he had heard nothing at all.

"Very well then," cried the imp, stamping his foot, "but you just wait till tomorrow!" and with that, he jumped back in the snuff-box.

When it was morning, the little boy ran to his toys and the first thing he saw was the Tin Soldier standing to attention on top of the table. Happily he played with his new toy but soon he could hear his mother calling him to breakfast. Then he very carefully placed the Tin Soldier on the window-sill until he returned.

Now whether it was the wind or whether the little black imp was

up to his tricks, I do not
know, but all at once
the window flew open
with a bang, the curtains
flapped and out fell
the little Tin Soldier,
tumbling head over
heels, from the third
storey nursery window!

That was a terrible fall
for the little Tin Soldier,
I can tell you! With a
bump he landed upside
down with his leg in
the air and there he
stayed, for his gun was
firmly wedged between
two paving-stones.

When the little boy returned and saw the window wide open and his favourite toy missing he guessed what had happened and quickly ran outside with the nursery-maid to search for the poor Tin Soldier.

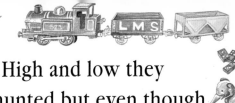

High and low they
hunted but even though
they were so close that
they almost trod on him,
still they did not see
him stuck upside down
between the paving
stones.

If the Tin Soldier had

only called out "Here I am!" they would have easily found him, but he could not bring himself to shout because he was wearing his smart uniform and he thought a soldier should be able to take care of himself.

Soon the sky grew grey and it began to drizzle. The raindrops fell faster and before long there was a regular steady downpour.

When the rain stopped, two little street urchins came along and soon they spotted the poor Tin Soldier.

"Just look!" cried one. "Here is a Tin Soldier! Let's make him a boat and then he shall sail up

and down like a fine Sea
Admiral of the Fleet!"
  So they made a little
boat out of newspaper
and the Tin Soldier
sailed up and down the
gutter whilst the boys
ran along beside him,
clapping their hands.

But what great waves there were in the gutter! The paper boat was tossed up and down and carried along so swiftly that the Tin Soldier trembled, but he remained steadfast and showed no fear.

All of a sudden the boat entered a long tunnel! The boys' excited cries faded away behind him with the light and soon it was just as dark as his box had been. "Where am I going now?"

wondered the little Tin Soldier. "Oh, dear! This is all the fault of that black imp! If only the little Dancer were sitting beside me here in the boat, it could be twice as dark for all I should care!"

Suddenly a great water rat poked his head out of the water alongside the paper boat and glared at the Tin Soldier.

"Have you a passport?" he demanded. "Come on — let me see your papers immediately!"

But the Tin Soldier never flinched. Silently he stared ahead and grasped his gun even more firmly than before.

The boat sped on down the dark tunnel with the huge rat swimming close behind.

Ugh! He was fierce and ugly and bared his sharp teeth as he called out to the scraps of rubbish floating along beside the boat. "Stop the Tin Soldier! Stop him! He has not paid the toll or shown his passport!"

The current in the water became swifter and stronger. Ahead of him the Tin Soldier was greatly relieved to see a glimpse of daylight at the end of the tunnel — but what was that terrible roaring noise?

He could hear the rushing of water, quite enough to frighten any brave man. Ahead of him the gutter emptied out into a great canal and for the poor Tin Soldier, that rush and tumble of water was just as dangerous as it would be for us to go headlong over a huge waterfall!

Now the water swirled so fiercely that he knew he could not last much longer. On rushed the boat as the water hissed

and boiled around him
and the noise grew ever
louder in his ears.

Suddenly the paper
boat whirled four times
around, and as the water
rushed in over its sides,
it began to sink! Then
the poor little Tin

Soldier stood straight to attention as best he could, for he wanted to be sure that no-one would ever be able to say afterwards that he had been a coward. There he stood, up to his neck in water, as the paper grew soggier and the boat sank deeper.

At last the cold water crept right over the top of his head and all he could think of was the pretty little Dancer whose face he should never see again.

As he sank into the murky depths he heard a voice inside his head.

"Forward, forward, soldier bold! Death's before thee, grim and cold!"

With that, the paper boat fell apart and the

soldier fell down, down — and at that moment was swallowed up by a great fish!

Oh! how dark it was inside the fish, even darker than it had been in the tunnel, and it was such a tight squash!

But there the steadfast little Tin Soldier lay full length, still shouldering his gun.

Up and down swam
the fish, then all at once
he began to twist and
thrash in the water. But
just as soon as he had
begun, the fish stopped
moving and became
quite still. The Soldier
lay quietly for a long

time, not knowing
where he was or what
would become of him.
Then like a flash of
lightning, bright
daylight streamed over
him, and a voice
exclaimed, "Why, here
is a little Tin Soldier!"

73

The Soldier had had quite a journey. The fish had been caught on a fisherman's hook, taken to market, sold, and was now lying silver-bright on a kitchen table ready to be cooked. What a surprise the

cook had when she saw
the Tin Soldier lying
ramrod straight in
the fish's belly, still
shouldering his gun!
She picked him up
between her finger and
thumb, and carried him
into the nursery, where

everyone wanted to see
the hero who had been
found inside a fish —
but the Tin Soldier did
not feel at all proud.

They put him on the
table, and — well, but
what strange things do
happen in this world!

The Tin Soldier was in
the very same room in
which he had once
shared a box with his
twenty four brothers!
He saw the same little
boy and there was the
same grand castle with
the pretty little Dancer.

She was still standing on one leg with the other high in the air, for she too was steadfast.

That moved the Tin
Soldier and he felt as if
he might shed tin-tears,
but that would not have
been fitting for a soldier.
He looked over at her,
and she looked straight
back at him, but she
said nothing.

All at once the little
boy picked up the Tin
Soldier and threw him
into the fire!

Why did he do it?
Nobody knew, but
doubtless the little black
imp in the snuff box
had something to do
with this new bit of
mischief, too.

There stood the Tin
Soldier, unflinching.

He balanced on his one leg right in the middle of the fire and the heat was truly terrible, but whether it was the pain of the flames or the pain of the love in his heart, he did not know for sure.

All his colour had worn off, and whether this had happened on his long journey or whether it was the result of his sorrow, who can say?

He looked straight at the little lady and she

looked straight at him, and he felt that he was melting, but still he remained steadfast, with his gun at his shoulder. Suddenly the door opened and a cold draught blew the little Dancer off the table.

She flew into the air
and floated just like
thistledown straight to
the Tin Soldier standing
steadfast in the fire and
as her arms brushed his
cheeks, she instantly
burst into flames. Then
the Tin Soldier finally

93

softened and began to melt in the hot flames.

Next morning when the maid came to clear away the ashes, she found a small lump of tin in the shape of a heart — all that was left of the little Tin Soldier.

And all that was left of the little Dancer was her golden rose, burnt as black as a cinder of coal.

HANS CHRISTIAN ANDERSON

Hans Andersen was born in Odense, Denmark on April 2nd, 1805. His family was very poor and throughout his life he suffered much unhappiness. Even after he had found success as a writer, Hans Andersen felt something of an outsider; an attitude which often emerged in his stories, such as here in *The Steadfast Tin Soldier*, published in 1838.

His fairy stories, famous throughout the world, include *The Snow Queen*, *The Little Mermaid* and *The Emperor's New Clothes*, and are amongst the most frequently translated works of literature.

He died in 1875.